This book
belongs to

....

To Mimi, with my love

GUMDROP'S
Magic Journey

Story and
pictures by
Val Biro

*Hodder
Children's
Books*

A division of Hodder Headline plc

MR JOSIAH OLDCASTLE was enjoying himself. He was driving Gumdrop and there was nothing he liked doing better than driving his trusty Austin Heavy 12/4, vintage 1926.

'This will be a mystery tour,' he announced to his grandson Dan. 'I have no plans or maps, so let's see where Gumdrop takes us!'

Gumdrop took them to an old-fashioned garage in the woods. 'What a sensible car,' exclaimed Mr Oldcastle, 'and anyway we need some petrol.'

The garage-man came out of the house. Dan thought that he
looked like a magician in some fairy tale. 'What a beautiful
vehicle,' said the man with a friendly smile. 'I've got just the
right petrol for your car and it will make your journey even
more interesting.'

Mr Oldcastle was glad to hear this, but he didn't notice the petrol
which now filled Gumdrop's tank. It was called SPELL. So he had
no inkling just *how* interesting their mystery tour would be!

He paid and they were off. Gumdrop shot forward like a car half his age. The garage-man looked on with satisfaction. 'The petrol is already working,' he thought, and smiled broadly.

But Mr Oldcastle had to slow down almost immediately, because a thick fog had suddenly descended. He switched on all the lights, but even so he could see no further than Gumdrop's thermometer. What's more, he could hear the engine of another car, approaching fast! So he honked Gumdrop's brass horn three times – and lo and behold, the fog lifted as if by magic!

The other car was an astonishing sight. Not because it was a veteran Darracq skidding and cavorting from side to side, but because it was driven by a toad. Yes, Toad himself! Mr Oldcastle was greatly surprised to meet him face to face. Dan had never heard of a toad driving a car, and he was enchanted.

Toad skidded to a halt and came running across. 'My dear Sir,' he said with his eyes nearly popping out, 'I have never seen such a magnificent motor-car as yours! What style! What grace! Oh my! Oh my!' He could hardly contain himself. In fact he offered there and then to swap his own car for Gumdrop, 'if you, Sir, and your young friend would be so obliging.'

Mr Oldcastle had just begun to say that he would never part with Gumdrop when he was interrupted by a loud clatter. They all looked round.

An old gentleman dressed as a white knight had just fallen off
his horse. Mr Oldcastle and Dan helped him back into the
saddle. His large mild eyes were still fixed on the Darracq.
'I fell off because I thought it was my own invention, but
then I recollected that I haven't invented the motor-car yet.'
And when he saw Gumdrop, he promptly fell off again.

Just then Toad noticed two small animals in a boat on the
river. 'Friends of mine,' he said with an embarrassed smile.
'Excellent fellows both, but just now I would rather not be
seen by Ratty or Mole.'
With which he tiptoed back to his
car, and, with another yearning look
at Gumdrop, he drove away.
The White Knight, who had managed
to remount, was seen riding away
and toppling off once more.

11

'This is magic!' cried Dan entranced. 'Where are we? Who are they? I want to see them again!' But Mr Oldcastle had no time to explain because a tortoise stood in the way, thumbing a lift.

'Thank you,' he said as he settled in Gumdrop, 'and if you happen to see a hare, please just drive on.' Sure enough they soon espied a hare who was sound asleep by the roadside. When he was left far behind, the tortoise got down with many thanks and plodded on towards what looked like the finishing-line of a race. 'I think that tortoise is cheating,' said Mr Old-castle, but he had no time to explain,

for suddenly he saw a lion running towards them. A lion! This was dangerous. He fought the steering-wheel to avoid a collision and Gumdrop skidded this way and that. 'Grandad!' yelled Dan. 'It's only an ass dressed as a lion!' But it was too late. Gumdrop skidded again and fell into the ditch.

'Now what?' exclaimed Mr Oldcastle. The distant roar of that lion was still in his ears, though actually it sounded like HEE-HAAW. 'How can we get Gumdrop out of here?'

'Allow me to help,' said a tall man, dismounting from his horse.
'I am the Baron Munchausen and am well-acquainted with such small
difficulties.' With which he placed Gumdrop, wheels and all,
upon his head and, climbing out of the ditch, he settled
the car gently back on the road again.
'Now let me tell you of a similar
adventure I've had back in Russia,'
said the Baron, and Dan was so
fascinated that they strolled
across the meadow, listening to
his incredible tales.

14

Meanwhile Gumdrop was not left standing alone for long.
Toad re-appeared in his car and stopped. He stared. Looked
all round. Saw no-one. Stared again. 'I wonder . . .' he
muttered as he crept across. Somehow he found
himself sitting in Gumdrop's driving-
seat. The engine started without
difficulty and the car moved forward, as if in a dream. 'Oh bliss!'
said Toad. 'Oh pooop-pooop!'
And he drove Gumdrop away
in a cloud of dust.

15

Mr Oldcastle heard the engine of his precious car and cam
running. 'It's that car-mad Toad again!' he yelled as he sav
the abandoned veteran car in place of Gumdrop. 'After
him!' He jumped into the Darracq with Dan and drove
off in hot pursuit. But there was no sign of Gumdrop, so
they stopped to ask two men who were walking near a palace. The
were weavers and they've never even heard of cars. 'But look at this
said one of that villainous pair. 'It is the miraculous cloth we've just wove
for the Emperor's new clothes!' And they held up the material – exce
that there was nothing in their hands. 'The Emperor will look funny in tha
said Dan, but Mr Oldcastle had no time for invisible clothes and drove o

Soon they reached a tumbledown cottage and stopped to ask if Gumdrop had been seen. 'No,' said the cross old woman who lived there with a cat and a hen. 'But you can take this ugly duckling away if you like!' And a young grey bird hopped straight into their car.

'Poor thing,' said Dan, 'he ought to be on the river.' And when they reached it, the bird flew straight out and he looked much happier. 'Anyway it's not a duckling . . .' began Dan but Mr Oldcastle had no time to explain, because . . .

. . . their way was blocked by seven little men marching along.
'No, we haven't seen Gumdrop,' said one of the dwarfs, a jolly
fellow. And we must hurry back home, otherwise Snow-White will
be cross if we are late for supper.' And they marched away, singing a
merry little song:

> Hey-ho, we worked all day,
> Ho-hey, we're on our way
> To Snow-White and supper and play.

'Snow-White?' asked Dan incredulously. 'Ugly Duckling? Where *are*
we, Grandad?' But Mr Oldcastle had no time to explain, because . . .

. . . suddenly they saw a funny little man dancing round a fire in front of his hut. He didn't notice the car and evidently thought that he was quite alone. As he danced he sang an odd little song:

> *Won't it be an awful mess*
> *And isn't it a dreadful shame*
> *How nobody will ever guess*
> *That Rumpelstiltskin is my name?*

And he cackled wickedly as he danced round and round.

'That's all very well,' complained Mr Oldcastle, 'but where *is* Gumdrop?' And he drove on as fast as he could.

19

In a while they reached a busy town. Suddenly a small boy leapt into their car. He had a long nose and he was made entirely of wood. He began to fiddle with the switches on the dashboard, he grabbed the steering-wheel and honked the horn. He was a very naughty boy.

An old man ran after them.
'Come back, Pinocchio! Come back!'
he panted. Pinocchio thereupon
leapt out and ran away. 'Stop
him! Stop him!' cried the old man
whose name was Geppetto.
Dan wished he could have run after Pinocchio and played
hide-and-seek with him, but Mr Oldcastle had turned the car and
was heading towards the country again. 'We must find Gumdrop,'
he growled, and drove the Darracq as fast as it would go.

21

Soon they came to a pleasant grove and stopped to read a notice pinned to a tree:

THIS WAY TO THE TEA PARTY

So they left the car and walked down to enquire about Gumdrop. A curious sight met their eyes.

A march hare and a hatter were having tea at a table, with a dormouse sitting between them, fast asleep.

'Have you seen Gumdrop hereabouts?' enquired Mr Oldcastle.
'What is Gumdrop?' asked the Mad Hatter, opening his eyes wide.
'Where is Hereabouts?' asked the March Hare as he poured a little tea upon the nose of the Dormouse.

Just as Mr Oldcastle prepared a suitable reply, he heard a sound.

HONK! HONK! The unmistakable sound of Gumdrop's curly brass horn! His heart leapt as he turned and raced back to the road.

And there stood dear old Gumdrop sure enough, safe and sound!
There also stood a miserable Toad between two constables. It took a
little while to explain that Gumdrop belonged to Mr Oldcastle and
how Toad had swapped it for his own car. It turned out that Toad
had stolen the Darracq as well! The Constables looked very stern.

'You are accused,' said
one of them to Toad, 'first,
of stealing two valuable motor-
cars, second, of driving to the
public danger and third, of gross
impertinence to the rural police.'
With which he formally arrested
the weeping Toad, ushered him into the waiting Darracq
and drove away to the Bench of Magistrates.

25

Mr Oldcastle and Dan climbed into Gumdrop with great joy and
turned to continue on their magic journey. But no sooner had they
gone half a mile when Gumdrop stopped – he had run out of petrol!
And at that moment a thick fog descended once again. Mr Oldcastle
remembered what to do and he honked Gumdrop's horn three times.
The fog lifted as if by magic. They found themselves back at
the old-fashioned garage in the woods.
Except that the garage and the petrol-pump had disappeared!

'I thought as much!' said Mr Oldcastle. 'The garage-man was Merlin the magician and he gave Gumdrop magic petrol. That's why our mystery tour had turned into a magic journey to Storyland!'

'Oh dear!' said Dan. 'Does it mean that the magic had run out with the petrol? Won't I meet those exciting people and animals ever again?'

'Not quite,' said Mr Oldcastle as he walked over to a table that appeared, as if by magic, where the petrol-pump had been. There was a pile of books on it, addressed 'To Dan'.

'You will meet them all again in these, my boy!'

27

And so he did.

He met the White Knight again in *Through the Looking Glass*,

the Hare and the Tortoise in *The Fables of Aesop*, (not forgetting the Ass Dressed as a Lion),

and he read all the incredible *Adventures of Baron Munchausen*. Dan found 'The Emperor's New Clothes' (which the weavers made) and 'The Ugly Duckling' in *Hans Andersen*,

and he read about the Seven Dwarfs and
wicked Rumpelstiltskin in *Grimm's Fairy Tales*.

The wooden boy and old Geppetto
lived in a book called *Pinocchio*,

and the mad tea party took place in *Alice's Adventures in Wonderland*.

And Toad? Why, he was as
large as life in *The Wind
in the Willows*, together
with Ratty and Mole.

And on most days since Gumdrop's magic journey, Dan can be seen sitting on the running-board, surrounded by his precious books. He is convinced that his new friends are all there too, and they seem as real to Dan as Gumdrop himself.

First published 1980
by Hodder & Stoughton Children's Books
This edition first published 1997 by
Hodder Children's Books,
a division of Hodder Headline plc,
338 Euston Road, London NW1 3HB.

Copyright © 1980 Val Biro

ISBN 0340 71455 7 Hardback
ISBN 0340 71441 7 Paperback

10 9 8 7 6 5 4 3 2 1

A catalogue record for this book is available from the British Library.
The right of Val Biro to be identified as the Author of this Work has been asserted by him.

Printed in Hong Kong